BLACK HEART METAL MONSTER
Michael Faun

DYNATOX MINISTRIES

Borneo – East Brunswick – Reseda

© 2013 Michael Faun

Published by
DYNATOX MINISTRIES
http://dynatoxministries.com

**ISBN-13:
978-1494304133
ISBN-10:
1494304139**

Thanks:

Jordan Krall for publishing this book and letting me pass through the Gates to Dynatox Ministries

Sophia Faun for cutting off the Rusty Chains

Alex S. Johnson for the Grim, Satanic Word-Wrangling and Hellish Edits

Jason Wayne Allen for placing the Keys before the Eye of the Gatekeeper

-Michael Faun, November 19th, 2013

Anulos qui animum ostendunt omnes gestemus!

PROLOGUE

Throatbutcher felt the blizzard of hellnotes surge through his blood. Wrapped in a cat-skin jacket—patches of smelly fur still clinging to it—he crawled up from a tomb at the center of the small stage, gripped the mic and made the curse stance. The frenzied audience, corpsepainted and straggle-haired teens, did the same in response.

By the time Nex's dissonant guitar-riff ended with a heavy blast beat (the cue for Throatbutcher's shrill howl) two giant black spider legs shot out from Throatbutcher's sunken eyes and impaled two fans at the front row, then retracted.

The blood droplets looked like miniature faces of Satan.

Happy with the unexpected presence of the Dark Prince, Throatbutcher turned to his band members to see their reactions. In slow motion he saw Ateranimus, Obscura Mortis' bass player, leer back at him with a strange expression etched on his pale barb-wired face. He suddenly stopped playing and picked up a grimy bucket of pigs blood standing by his amplifier.

Nex, absorbed in rapid guitar shredding, didn't even notice the lack of bass, or the fact that Ateranimus had emptied the bucket over his head.

A low frequency WHOOOM thundered throughout the small venue. Electric sparks rained like blue-white hail from Ateranimus, who toppled over and lay convulsing. Smoke smelling of burned hair and skin spread like a slow fog among the audience.

The fans made the sign of the horns.

Skinreaper, the batterist, threw his sticks and leaped over his drum set, trying desperately to signal to the technicians to kill the power.

They weren't there.

Panic-stricken, he looked around the foggy stage, trying to find some kind of emergency switch. There weren't any.

By now, only the guitar and a playback synth playing fast diabolical melodies were heard over the audience's enthusiastic whistles and shouts.

Throatbutcher dropped the microphone and staggered toward the backstage door, where he tripped over a coffin-shaped stomp box. Falling like a tree, he landed on his head. White pom-poms of pain flashed before his eyes, shutting off half his brain and switching on the drug-fuelled auto-pilot.

The acid-spiked goat blood he had been shooting up before the gig (last one on their Ancient Mass Tour) now raged with potency. Throatbutcher was transforming into a half-spider, half-goat, with spiraling lead horns harpooning out from his melting skull. He tried to crawl the last bit to the door, but couldn't move.

Deep mocking laughter echoed from somewhere.

Before passing out, two mental notes floated up in his fuzzy head:

1) Inform the band about his new stage name: Spiderbutcher.

2) Ask manager Tabitha for more of that fantastic drug.

CHAPTER ONE

Each toll of the church-bell was like a sock in the faces of the remaining trio of Obscura Mortis. Standing by the fringe of the misty autumn forest, they witnessed the offensive Christian burial of their late bass player Ateranimus, or Øyvind Amundsen which had been his real name. His white coffin was slowly being lowered into a damp earth pit.

Gathered around the six-feet-deep hole, were a handful of mourners. Ateranimus' balding father, Bjørkefjord's own priest, conducted the ignominy. Reading aloud from Bibelen and crossing himself, he showed no sign of grief.

Tabitha had pulled every possible string to arrange a Satanic funeral for Ateranimus. An endeavor which had proven impossible, and only deepened the hate-relation between the band and the villagers of the deeply religious town of Bjørkefjord—Ateranimus' place of birth, and later, also the heart and musical nerve center of Obscura Mortis, who collectively lived and recorded in a red house not far from town. Deep in the dark Norwegian pine tree forest.

Two years earlier, Throatbutcher and Nex were on the hunt for a bass player and a batterist to form a band. The two had sent around a bunch of demos to every musician active in Norway's black metal scene. Within a week, they had been contacted by Øyvind who said he was mighty impressed with the demo. He thought their music possessed a whole new level of darkness and originality and he wanted to try out for the bass player position.

Psyched about the guy's attitude towards their music, they arranged to meet him and were blown away by the news that he owned a house, and had even built a studio in the cellar.

Without thinking twice, Throatbutcher and Nex packed their gear (a bag of rare black metal records, knives, and a case of beer) and driven out to the house in Bjørkefjord, thirty miles West of their own town, Skjærfjord.

The stars were right, the chemistry flawless. That very same night they recorded a three track EP, together with their newfound bass player Øyvind—who took the moniker Ateranimus—in his studio.

They named the EP *Ancient Mass*. Ateranimus painted the crude cover art picturing a stripped nun penetrated by a smoldering inverted cross. Her facial expression was lewd and a strand of drool hung from her quivering lip. A smoking pentagram holding the EP's title was burn-marked on her forehead.

* * *

Throatbutcher flipped open his Zippo and lighted a cigarette. "Know what we should do?" Inhaling deeply, he narrowed his eyes and stared furiously at the undignified ceremony.

Nex nodded and drank from a pentagram-engraved silver flask before passing it over to Throatbutcher. Wiping his mouth with the sleeve of his leather coat, he suddenly squealed as one of the five inch spikes accidentally got in his eye. "Ouch, fucking shit!" His hands flew to his eye as he spun around and stomped his boots on some pine cones.

Throatbutcher ignored his friend's fit. His eyes were somewhere far away. "We should build ourselves a bunch of those homemade bombs, you know? With nuts and bolts and whatnot. Hell, even throw in some crosses! And place one under each of those graves," he air-jabbed the distant headstones with his cigarette fingers, "then hit the button and boom, the world's greatest exhuming!" Throatbutcher snickered and took a good slug of booze.

Skinreaper, who had been rather quiet since the night of Ateranimus' live performance sacrifice, stood leaning over one of the shovels they had brought for their mission, or, liberation, as it was referred to by the other two.

This is really fucked up, he thought and nodded his concurrence with Throatbutcher's wise words. A sick feeling was growing inside him. "Did anyone mention this to Tabitha?" he asked, arching a brow.

The question drew Nex's immediate attention. His corpsepaint was old and flaked, making him look somewhat like an evil dying panda. Suddenly his arm shot out and he took a steady grip of Skinreaper's shoulder. Staring at him with his spiked blue eye, his braided coppery beard swayed like a hairy pendulum under his jutting jaw. "Why, you fucking her or something?"

"What? No!"

If you only knew what things Tabitha and I did on your amp last week!

Skinreaper returned the evil eye, standing his ground. But something in Nex's intimidating stare made him tip his head back, as if the man's eyes possessed a force field pushing it that way. He shrugged out of Nex's claw-like grip.

Throatbutcher broke out in his usual hoarse laughter. The maniacal joy dwindled down to a chuckle. "Didn't she tell you?" He flicked his cig against a tree, sending a cascade of orange glow raining to the ground. "This was all her idea, told us to meet up with her at the house afterwards. Said she had good news."

"Oh? Ok. Cool." Skinreaper was surprised. She usually revealed all band related news to him before telling the others. He bored his fingers hard into his palm. *Had she, too, gone mad with the whole Satanist business?*

"Hey, look, they're leaving," Nex cut in. "Let's do some digging." His focus had shifted from Skinreaper's shoulder to the little graveyard by the church not fifty yards away. He clumsily moved about and grabbed a shovel.

"About fucking time," Throatbutcher wheezed and yanked his shovel up from the frosty ground. "Time to take back what they stole from us." He patted Nex's back and winked at Skinreaper before taking the lead out of the forest. Dry twigs and pine cones crunched under his boots.

Nex followed next. Last out from the fringe was Skinreaper who, stomach knotting, swallowed once and glanced out over the calm burial ground. He deeply wished he had left this band already.

Dusk was creeping in quickly. A cold reddish glow lay like a lid over the graveyard and its twenty-some headstones. Sacred ground now trespassed on by an unholy alliance. All wearing makeup that made them look like living dead.

Throatbutcher's shovel was first to dig into the freshly laden soil atop Ateranimus' casket. "Don't worry, buddy," he whispered. "You're coming back home with us now."

Skinreaper documented the desecration with his camera.

Nex urinated on Ateranimus' flower adorned tombstone…

CHAPTER TWO

Tabitha's dark blue Honda skidded to a halt outside the only Texaco station in Skjærfjord. It was late afternoon and the rain was transforming the black red and white neon sign into a dark square blur behind the drenched windshield.

She climbed out and grabbed the pump she had parked by, flipped open the ice-cold gas cap and stuck the pipe in it with a hollow clonk. The meter began ticking. She couldn't wait to get to the house, excited to reveal the plans to the band.

Her mind then wandered away to Skinreaper and their last little rendezvous. It brought a naughty grin to her face.

Pulling out the pump, she hurried into the station shop to pay. The door bell jangled cheerfully. A sound totally un-matching the look on the face of the guy behind the counter.

"Hello there," Tabitha greeted with an enigmatic smile. She adjusted her tight black SATAN LOVES ME dress, pulled out a bundle of cash from her shredded stockings and began counting the amount she owed for the gas.

The clerk didn't greet her back. Tabitha got the impression he was a dwarf or a really short person since his chubby, blond-peppered chin rested on the smooth surface of the counter.

He looked at Tabitha with the eyes of a Ku Klux Klan member looking at their sworn enemy. A mix of hate and fear.

"That'll be thirty Crowns," he said through pursed lips. His voice was cautious yet had an air of challenge in it.

Tabitha folded the money and handed them to him. She then noticed he wasn't a dwarf after all, but a man in a wheelchair. Both legs missing. He had nothing left from the crotch down save for the loose bright jeans hanging over the seat like a shapeless denim curtain.

She suddenly realized she was grimacing.

The disabled clerk saw her reaction. He was used to the consternated look by now and quite amused by freaked out customers, so he simply grinned, saying, "Aren't you the manager for...what's their name now again...oh yeah—Obscura Mortis?"

"Yes!" Tabitha answered way too fast and way too high pitched. Her face turned red. Filled with embarrassment, her eyes shot to the counter candy rack from where she grabbed some gum. "You listen to them?"

Stupid question! Guy's physically challenged and is dressed like a muppet. Not the typical black metal fan...

"Me? Oh, no, just curious." He took the cash laying on the counter, fed them to the register and let out a strained chuckle. "I recall some of the band members used to live here before. Guess they moved. Must've become quite famous after that suicide on stage..."

"Oh, you mean *the sacrifice*. Yes. They did." Tabitha frowned. The weird vibe of the conversation irritated her. She had no time to stand here yapping with a retard. "You can keep the change." She arched her brow and turned, popping a mint gum into her mouth as she strutted out from the bright lit shop.

Just as the sliding doors swished open at the exit, the clerk suddenly addressed her again. "Are you going to their house now?"

A cold tickle ran along her spine. Choosing to ignore it, she left, shaking her head.

Driving off in the thick gray rain, she peeked into the rearview mirror. She saw the strange clerk wheel himself out from the station shop. Stopping by one of the pumps, he watched her take the road North to Bjørkefjord.

CHAPTER THREE

Throatbutcher and Nex struggled with Ateranimus' corpse as they carried it up the stairs of the red house. Tabitha was already on the second floor, standing by the door to Ateranimus' room. In the vestibule, Skinreaper locked the front door and shook his wet hair. It had started raining the second their shovels scooped up the grave and the smell of the now soaked, dirt-ridden corpse was now spreading in their house.

Skinreaper stole a glance at Tabitha who had a megalomaniacal grin on her face. She was carefully conducting the transportation of Ateranimus' body, waving her thin arms like a traffic cop.

"Okay, guys, aaaalmost there, only two more steps. Careful, careful with his head..." she said.

Throatbutcher and Nex were groaning and panting, the narrow stairs creaking from their collected weight.

"There. Perfect." Tabitha made way. "Haul him in and lay him on his bed. Then we'll begin the ritual."

"Damn, could you do my room next?" Throatbutcher, who was first man inside the room, sounded impressed. Nex whistled as he entered.

"I thank thee." Tabitha tilted her head and offered a theatrical smile along with a courteous hand gesture.

"Whoa," Skinreaper silently mouthed as he peeked into Ateranimus' dim room. On the bed, over a black satin sheet with a white embroidered pentagram, Ateranimus' waxy body was placed in a position to match the five pointed symbol. Like a morbid version of Da Vinci's "The Vitruvian Man".

By the headboard, a three feet high inverted crucifix had been welded to the headboard. Dozens of black candles surrounded the bed. Their nail sized flames, still and feeble, steamed up the single window in the room.

While the others were busy setting up the ritual, Skinreaper's eyes wandered to the ceiling. There, right above the bed, a dead goat dangled, its jaw tied to some wires jutting from the empty lamp socket.

"Don't just stand there. Get inside and shut the door." Tabitha said eagerly.

Skinreaper felt nervous. His lips were dry, his heart racing. This was it. A *real* Satanic ritual. His first. And hopefully last. He didn't believe in this shit for real. For him it was more of a gimmick. Make believe. And even though he was used to the usual black metal stuff by now—dead dismembered animals, smelly bone necklaces, and gallons of animal blood emptied into dirty plastic drums—this felt like it had gone too far.

I'm in this shit too deep. Just play along with it and everything will be cool.

Skinreaper leered as he got into the stuffy room and closed the door behind him. The before characteristic, musty birch smell was gone. Replaced, by the stench of death and insanity. He kneeled by the bed and lowered his head like the others.

Tabitha began reading aloud from a document, stretching out every syllable and voicing it in a strange high pitch, "Nil igitur mors est ad nos neque pertinet hilum, quandoquidem natura animi mortalis habetur."

Despite the off-putting situation, Skinreaper found her chanting humorous. She sounded like a horror TV-show presenter from the 60's—or a yowling cat in the rutting season.

Throatbutcher and Nex blindly repeated the Latin verse.

Skinreaper, with no skills in Latin, just murmured along. The silence afterwards, though, made his skin crawl. It was as if the house's woodwork was responding to the ritual. Moving and creaking.

"Lucifer's child has now returned to his eternal bedchambers." Tabitha closed her eyes and took a deep breath, exhaled and opened her eyes, marking the end of the funeral rite.

As everybody slowly rose to their feet, Tabitha, back in her normal voice, said, "We want you to record a tribute EP. Starting tonight." Her oakish eyes glittered in the dark. "I've stacked the studio fridge with all you guys need. Plus," she winked at Throatbutcher, "I've scored some of that special stuff you requested down there, too."

The gloomy atmosphere inside that death chamber instantly changed. Throatbutcher and Nex were psyched, immediately spitting out musical and visual ideas.

Skinreaper's angst lifted. A smile was even forming on his parched lips.

We'll just have to put Ateranimus back in his grave and then it's like this never happened. I could live with that.

"Well, I'll leave you guys alone so you can begin your creative process immediately." Tabitha beamed like a mother. "Call me the minute you've finished the raw tracks. I can't wait to hear what you'll cook up!"

They left the room and headed down to the vestibule where Tabitha wished them luck; hugging them all before she left the house. When nobody was looking, she squeezed Skinreaper's ass.

On the way down to the cellar studio, Throatbutcher, Nex and Skinreaper were all fired up. For the first time since Ateranimus' demise, they felt like a band again.

Meanwhile, up on the second floor, a starving white mouse—relieved that the party had finally left—scurried out from a hole behind a shelf. Its red pearly eyes glittered the feast of meat they had left behind. The small claws were clicking against the metal bed frame as it easily climbed up and began to nibble on Ateranimus.

First, the moist skin of his face, to work up an appetite. Then, as main coarse, his throat, where it gnawed up a jagged hole and ravenously began to chew the flesh inside. Viscous semi-clotted blood began to glop out like blackish-red slush. Slowly marinating the floorboards underneath the bed...

CHAPTER FOUR

The huge wall-fan inside the small record shop, The Black Wax Tomb, droned so loud it nearly killed the Venom album playing. Even worse of an insult was the stink of kebab polluting the fresh smell of plastic on every vinyl record.

Nex hated it. In fact, he wanted to burn the place down. But "Gravene" was the only place to buy records in Skjærfjord so that wasn't a smart idea.

He perused the plastic jackets stacked in the old beer crates. Eyes mechanically scanning the turgid white spidery logos for new 7-inches. All while thinking of ways to murder the chubby poser behind the counter. No true disciple of black metal chose a wall fan over *Welcome to Hell*. To Nex, this was a kind of Satanic blasphemy.

Maybe he could bash his egg-shaped head in, using his brand new morning star.

The poser had dyed his blond hair black. Poorly, so that the light hair shone through. He looked like a faggy mutant version of a tubby medieval page. Dressed in too big black pants and a brand-new Dimmu Borgir t-shirt. A pathetic joke.

"Yes..." Nex suddenly whispered as he carefully pulled up the sleeve and held it up. His eyes were burning like dark torches as they beheld the album: Darkthrone's *Under a Funeral Moon*.

Nex's friend Engelhard, visual artist and black metal aficionado, would definitely be green of envy over his find and buy several rounds of booze just for a cassette copy when they met up for beers later.

Nex snickered at the thought and headed toward the counter. His black leather coat squeaked and chains were rattling.

The poser who was reading a fanzine. He didn't look a day over sixteen, and didn't dare to meet Nex's eyes. His fumbling fingers discarded the flimsy fanzine onto a little side table, also holding a soda with a straw.

He cleared his throat as Nex slid the record at him.

The clerk took a closer look at the price sticker. "Ahem, that'd be ninety. And if you have one of these,"—he produced a black paper 2x8 card with empty slots on it—"you get a stamp for each buy for fifty or more, and after your tenth, you receive a free--"

"I only want the album." Nex reached for the chain attached to his wallet in his back pants-pocket. With a quick yank, the wallet flew out and landed perfectly in his palm.

The poser tapped his fingers on some flyers, leaving greasy smudges on the ink.

Nex frowned and began feeling for some cash.

There were none.

He suddenly remembered that he'd spent his last cash on paper scratchers last night. When he was drunk.

"Shit," he muttered. He slowly put his wallet back in his pocket. Scratching his scraggly red peppered chin, he grinned. "Um, could you set it aside for me for tomorrow? Forgot to bring money."

The clerk squirmed in his seat, his face turning red. "I'm sorry, but I can't do that. It's shop policy." His drumming fingers had now climbed to a thrash beat.

"Shop policy?" Nex raised his brows. "But, I said I'll be in *tomorrow?* Maybe you didn't get that, with all the noise from that fucking blower!" He pointed angrily at the World War Two-type apparatus steadily rotating behind the counter like a cement mixer on the fritz, greedily sucking in the rat meat stench from the kebab place next door.

"Y-Yes, I heard that." Poser's palms flew up in defense. "Look, I'm really sorry but I can't help it. It's shop policy..." The clerk was rocking back and forth now. "It's not that I don't trust you...only that people never come back like they say, and you know..." His voice dwindled down into nothing. Only the fan pumping hard behind.

Nex wanted to demolish the poser's fat face. Plant a spiked knuckle into his beady little eye. But he didn't. Not now.

"Well, you know what, you little poser?" Nex snorted and drew a hand through his hair, "You can be absolutely fucking sure I'm one of the people who *will* be back!" Balling his hand into a fist, he knocked over a carton of cheap demo cassettes that exploded against the chequered tile floor; creating a mess of cassette cases and brown tapeworm.

Nex stormed out of the Black Wax Tomb, slamming the door behind him.

A little bell tinkled in mockery...

* * *

Skjærfjord was not a metropolis, but it had everything a man needed. At least, that was Nex's opinion. He was a simple man. Didn't care for beauty salons, or fancy boutiques, or big malls with espresso bars in them, or none of that other homo stuff. There was the Black Wax Tomb, Bjørnulf's Burger Hut, a Texaco, lots of dark forest woods and of course, Røde Viking Bar & Grill—where he spent almost every night of the week.

Vikingene, as people called it, was—quite obviously—a Viking-themed restaurant, nautical designed with small wooden huts and fishing nets hanging down from the ceiling. Rune-engraved shields were fastened on the walls, and by the door stood a large red-bearded Viking statue, welcoming the patrons with a grim, haggard look.

The place had a ground level and a basement. First was the dining area where Skjærfjord's middle class denizens spent the evenings after work, filling their flabby bellies with fish and fine wine. Then there was the basement, much smaller, dimly lit and strictly reserved for Skjærfjord's drunks, poisoning their livers with cheap wine and beer.

At least until Skjærfjord's mischief youth, the black metal pack had found out about it and driven the winos out, making it their place. It was now the natural hub for the growing scene. Bands were formed there, demos were peddled, and copious amounts of alcohol were consumed.

This Friday night, the place was packed. Diabolical shrill melodies blared from the cheap corner speakers and laughs. Loud conversation hung thick in the smoky air. Nex sipped the beer he had put on his ever-growing tab, still pissed about the incident over at 'Gravene' earlier that afternoon.

Finally, through the mist of the cigarette smoke, came Engelhard. Treelike and skinny, he strode toward Nex's booth. He had the sly grin of a wolf lurking by a corral of lambs.

Nex noticed the black plastic bag he was carrying. It was slim and had vinyl in it. Engelhard sat down in

Nex's booth and put down the bag of records on the table between them.

"Hey there, what's up?" Engelhard asked as a waitress suddenly appeared with two beers she put down between them. The blonde girl in a Bathory shirt winked at Engelhard who smiled back like a little boy.

Nex sighed, gave Engelhard a hard eye and restlessly clinked his pentagram ring against his beer bottle. He slugged down the last of his old beer and glanced curiously at the bag of vinyl. "What've you got there?"

Engelhard, whose eyes were on the waitress' ass, snapped out from his mesmerized stare and drank from his green bottle. "Oh, some new shit and some old shit. Finally got Darkthrone's latest. Man, was that hard to come by!"

Chagrined, Nex jammed his hand into the bag and whipped out a fat stack of 7-inch EP's and some full lengths. A strong waft of plastic oozed up from the vinyl jackets.

"Oh, yes, there it is." Engelhard proudly announced, pointing with the beer at the album Nex was gloating at. *Under a Funeral Moon.* "My brain was nearly exploding when I found it. You wanna rip it?"

Nex felt divided. He had found the record first. *And if it hadn't been for the fucktard behind the counter...*

His hands were clammy just holding it.

"Yeah," Nex muttered. "Saw this earlier today." His voice sounded distant.

"You did? Why the hell didn't you buy it? You've been talking about it for months!?" Engelhard looked baffled. He took another slug, shooting a glance over the booths for familiar faces. "Slow night tonight, huh."

Nex gritted his teeth. "I *was* going to buy it. But I spent my last fucking money on stupid shit last night after all those Jaeger shots. The fat poser bitch refused to lay it aside for me. Swear I'm gonna' smash his fucking face in next time I see him." Nex put back the plastic treasure into the bag. "I'm taking a piss."

He darted up from his seat and headed toward the restroom in the back. The swinging door slammed open as he rammed his leather-fitted elbow into it.

As he stood there peeing in the urinal, cursing silently, the door to the restroom suddenly creaked open. Nex recognized the emaciated guy coming in as one of the regulars. He had a big Burzum patch attached to the breast of his leather jacket.

He undid his bullet belt and whipped out his dick. Tinkling squirts hit against the urinal wall, followed by a groan of relief.

Both stood in silence, making sure to avoid any form of eye-contact.

The dude with the Burzum patch suddenly addressed Nex with a drawling hoarse voice, "Shame about the Darkthrone album. Definitely their best yet."

Nex wasn't sure if the guy was provoking him or tried to start up a friendly conversation. Either case, he decided to see where it would lead. Tonight of all nights, he wouldn't mind burying his fist in somebody's face. Burzum patch or not.

"What?" Nex asked. Still no eye-contact between them. The code of two men urinating next to each other.

No reply. The guy pulled up his pants and bucked his belt. "Been having some issues with that fat cunt myself lately. Refused to let me put up a band ad in there last week."

Nex flied his zipper, and since both men's dicks were in, he finally looked at him and said, "Yeah? What a fucking asshole." The two of them began to lug toward the door. Finally, some shared hatred. "So, I take it you play? Anything I've heard?"

"Nah, just toying around with a solo project at the moment. Throating my guts out to some guitar and synth drums. I'll throw you a demo if you want." The guy laughed as he opened the door. It sounded like coarse sandpaper against gravel.

Nex let out a friendly chuckle. "Maybe we could start something up. I'm a guitarist looking to form a band. Have lots of ideas."

"Who knows?" The guy threw a cryptic smirk as the two walked toward their respective booths.

"I'm Nex by the way."

"Throatbutcher." He offered his bony hand and Nex shook it. "Want a beer?"

"Sure, man, thanks!"

They came up to the bar and Throatbutcher bought two fresh beers and two vodka shots. He said in a low voice, "Hey, I was thinking, later tonight, we should give the fat cunt a little fright. You game?"

Nex downed his shot, loving what he heard. "What did you have in mind?"

A devilish grin spread over Throatbutcher's gaunt face.

* * *

Not even the roaring engine of the black Nissan, nor Darkthrone, could drown the terrified screams coming from the Black Wax Tomb poser who was tied to a pine-tree by the fringe of the forest. A full yellow moon hung high up in the onyx sky. The poser's face, wet with tears, was brilliantly exposed in the white beam of the headlights not ten yards away.

Throatbutcher clutched the wheel and Nex rode shotgun, both guffawing like two mad gulls each time Throatbutcher revved the engine, sending the back tires spinning, flinging up dirt. Then he released the handbrake.

The car lurched forward like an angry bee. Nex yelled with delight. The guy tied to the tree closed his eyes and turned his head away, writhing like a snake in a jar as the car cannonballed ahead.

"Fucking hell," growled Throatbutcher, too drunk to stop the car in time. A sickening howl sounded as the car's front smashed into the guy's lower body; spattering the windshield with blood.

Throatbutcher and Nex's heads slammed against the front panel in the collision. The horn blared. The motor was coughed. Throatbutcher put the car in reverse and the cries climbed in pitch.

Heads pounding, they drove away as the song "Inn i De Dype Skogers Favn" butchered the stereo speakers. Darkthrone's new album was indeed a masterpiece.

CHAPTER FIVE

*B*LIP

REC 93/10/07 02:44

A red led lamp lit up as Skinreaper pressed the REC button on the handycam. The first thing seen through the lens was Nex, lying like a wreck on a worn black leather sofa. A low glass table stood beside him; cluttered with beer bottles and crumpled cash notes next to a mound of white powder.

A fast black metal riff played at a deafening level in the background. Skinreaper's stoned chuckle could be heard over the three evil-sounding notes.

He circled, filming the entire cellar studio. Amps, guitars, a filled goat skull ashtray and animal horns flashed by the shaky image before finally zooming in on the glass window. The song booth. Throatbutcher's bird-like silhouette growled into a microphone, repeating the question, "How does the Dark Prince achieve the unruly death?"

Skinreaper started speaking into the camera mic. "Hey…it's the middle of the night and we're in the studio still. Um…think we're on day three now, and so far we've laid down the base tracks for two of four songs for the Ateranimus tribute EP."

He coughed and cleared his throat.

"As you just saw, Nex has passed out and…if you just hold on…you may be lucky enough to witness Throatbutcher have his regular fit. Man, is he in some hocus-pocus state! Courtesy of our generous and creative manager who supplied him with some of that evil substance, hehehe.

"The riff you hear in the background has been playing over and over and over for...um...five hours now, and he's been rambling the same verse line all that time. Think his head is about to explode any time now...just watch!"

The camera zoomed in so close on Throatbutcher's corpse painted face, you could see the grease paint cracking up from the vocalist's sweat.

Throatbutcher stopped singing. He slowly turned his head and stared straight into the lens. His crazy white eyes glinted in the shadows.

"Oh shit!" Skinreaper cried. The camera image made a hasty jerk as he backed away and—Throatbutcher drove his mic-stand straight trough the glass shield, sending a torrent of sharp splinters tinkling down onto the wooden floor. Waving and thrashing, he howled in fury, barging out from the cramped space toward the camera. He brandished the mic-stand in midair like a Norse warrior crazed on mushrooms.

The camera image tumbled aimlessly. Fast thumping footsteps and aggressive yelling. The very last thing that was caught on tape was a drawn-out creaking coming from the woodworks. As if the house were moaning.

Then the camera shut off.

CHAPTER SIX

The glaring neon signs inside Bjørnulf's Burger Hut were hard on a hangover. Even worse were the frantic Jerry Lee Lewis songs constantly playing through the budget jukebox.

Throatbutcher, Nex and Ateranimus were sitting in the 1950's Americana-themed diner by a corner table cluttered with plates of greasy food, stuffing their faces and chit-chatting. Tabitha was going to introduce them to some drummer.

Ateranimus snorted, drowning his fries in a river of Tabasco. He shoved a handful into his mouth, pointing his finger at Nex. "Heard Tabitha dumped you at the Underbelly yesterday?" He chewed his fries faster, a smirk on his lips.

Dissecting a burnt chicken wing, Throatbutcher let out a hoarse snicker.

"Says who?" Nex arched his brow and drank from his soda. In three big slugs, he emptied the can and let out a rumbling burp. His mind darkened but he kept his cool, determined to twist last night's embarrassment to his advantage. No way was he going to let Tabitha ruin his rep.

Since the day Obscura Mortis signed with Sulfur Pit Records, Nex had nursed a flame for the band's manager. Tabitha was his kind of girl: twig-thin, into Satanism and hooked on coke. She also had an ass that would make Lucifer cry. And black velvet hair reaching down to that amazing ass. Nex wanted that bad.

At the party held for the band that same night, while the rest of the band (then including their previous drummer Johan who immediately was kicked out of the band after Nex had found Whitesnake's single "Is This Love" sticking out from one of his cymbal cases) had gotten shit-faced in the witching hour, Nex had been busy stuffing Tabitha's X-Mas socket in the company President's upstairs office; doing lines of coke on her pale ample tits.

From that night on, things had snowballed.

It wasn't like they were a couple or nothing. Their relationship was purely sexual. Still, Nex was confused over the fact that she, just the other night, had simply walked up to him and said she wanted to end everything between them (except the business part). Then she had just left the Underbelly. Had she found a new play buddy? The image of some other dude sticking his python into her snake pit kept grinding inside Nex's head.

That cold-hearted bitch...

"Nobody," Ateranimus replied. "But I saw her leave with some other guy. A short beefy dude. Think he's Corpsebeater's batterist. Figured she'd dumped you for him."

"Oh, that guy, Skinreaper. Isn't he gay?" Nex took a big chew of his chili burger, savoring the spicy flavor as it mixed with the anger building in his throat. "Well, no. She didn't dump me. I told *her* that I wanna fuck other chicks besides her and she couldn't take it so she freaked out and left. Guess she needed a shoulder to cry on."

"Speaking of the devil..." Throatbutcher wheezed and nodded toward the entrance.

"Hey, and she's with the comforting shoulder." Ateranimus chuckled and winked at Nex.

Tabitha's loud laughter suddenly invaded Bjørnulf's Burger Hut. Nex gloated at the guy she came in with. Short. Beefy. Fitted Ateranimus' description to the tee. A cocksure grin was etched on his pinkish haughty face framed by thick black hair.

What the hell? Dude looks like a fucking pig!

"Hi guys!" Tabitha cheerily greeted while prancing in and sitting down by their table. She dodged Nex's eyes. "Meet your new possible drummer. I've just heard him play and I'm telling you, this guy knows how to work his sticks." She blushed as her words came out.

I bet he does, you slut.

The pig was standing by her side, finger drumming on his pants and nodding coolly at the three band members. "Hey, heard your stuff. It's great. I'm Skinreaper. So, heard about that shit with Johan. Whitesnake? Seriously? Who would've thought?"

"Yeah..." Throatbutcher muttered. He and Ateranimus introduced themselves. Nex acknowledged his presence with a light nod and a forced smile.

"Thought you played with Corpsebeater?" Ateranimus frowned and shoveled more fries into his mouth.

"I did. Quit the other week, though. Didn't get along anymore. Long story." Skinreaper ordered some beers and joined the others at the table. The conversation bloomed into a lively discussion about the black metal scene in general, complete with the obligatory namedropping and musical influences, bands they all dug (some of which Skinreaper had even toured with), plus local rumors.

Throatbutcher and Ateranimus seemed to hit it off with the new guy. Tabitha, too, laughed at his jokes and batted her lashes when he mentioned some crazy shit he had done at gigs.

Nex mostly sat quiet, focusing on his chili-burger. He'd chalked up the guy as yet another poser. He didn't speak his mind though. Instead, he just nodded at the right moments. Now and then trying to make eye contact with Tabitha.

It was like trying to get the attention of a concrete wall.

After some beers, they decided to drive out to the house and try out the Skinreaper's drumming skills.

* * *

"So, what do you guys say?" Tabitha spewed out a plume of smoke toward the high ivory moon. The band stood outside the house, sharing a bottle of bourbon and smoking cigarettes.

Tabitha's hand was resting on her hip and she had a twinkle in her eye. "He good or what?"

Nex snorted, hocked up a loogie and drank greedily from the flask going around. He waited for someone else to answer.

Throatbutcher and Ateranimus stood peering out at the pointy tree tops of the dark pine forest, contemplating.

"I think he kicked ass," Throatbutcher said hoarsely. He fired up another smoke, took a deep drag and continued as he exhaled, "Grinded the shit out of every song on Ancient Mass. I think we should keep him. For me it's a yes." He slapped his arm against his side to get warm, raising a brow to the others.

"Can he beat the skins? No question about it. Does he fit in?" Nex shrugged and kicked some gravel. "Not sure..." He yawned and rubbed some dust in his eye. "You decide..."

"Mmmkay?" Tabitha said, arching a brow.

You fucking child.

She shot an expectant look at Ateranimus.

"Hell yes! I'll second Throatbutcher. I really dug what he did on 'Beastly Ejaculation'." Ateranimus grinned and unleashed his black hair from the rubber band. "Tight as hell. Plus, I really leveled with him basswise. I say, let's welcome him into the band so we could get that damn tour going already. Man, I wanna tour!"

"Yaay!" Tabitha burst out. "I'll go tell the good news and get his contract fixed up pronto. We'll meet you at the Underbelly after."

Nex glanced at her. "Oh, we can wait. We'll hit the place together. Like a *band*." His words came out a little too strained.

"Oh, come on, man, I'm thirsty. Let's roll," Throatbutcher whined. He and Ateranimus were already footing toward the black Nissan parked by the country road.

Nex felt a pang of frustration. He turned and dragged his feet to the idling car from which Darkthrone's "To Walk the Infernal Fields" blared from the speakers.

"Cool, catch you guys later," Tabitha said and killed her cigarette with the high heel of her shoe. Humming the chorus of the Darkthone song, she hurried back into the house. She could feel Nex's eyes burning her back, and she loved it.

During the short descent down to the cellar studio, erotic stirrings tingled in Tabitha's groin. Skinreaper played drums the way he fucked: fast and hard.

* * *

"I'm in!?" Skinreaper cried, hoisting up Tabitha, wrapped around him like a second skin, onto Nex's Marshall amp. He pulled up her black skirt with his hand, tugging at her fishnet stockings. Her body bucked in response.

"Sure are," Tabitha whispered in his ear. "Now, how will you reward me?" She began licking his ear and rubbing her moist panties against his groin. Skinreaper instantly hardened and worked his hand up to her ample tit, massaging it hard while thumbing its stiff nipple. "You're so fucking hot," he groaned.

"So, just fuck me already," Tabitha teased. She bit his ear and threw her head back, letting her long hair fall like a black tidal wave. She moaned as his other hand, the one not squeezing her tit, began exploring her southern mountain top. "Just don't tell the others about us, Nex'd kill us if he knew."

"Don't worry, I—"

A sudden bang came from the staircase. Skinreaper spun around in an awkward motion, quickly zipping his pants.

Wincing, Tabitha pulled down her skirt and jumped off the amplifier. Her face was flushed, her breathing fast.

They looked like two kids caught red-handed while making out in the school bathroom.

Silently, Tabitha trotted over to the cellar door that stood ajar, and peered up the staircase.

"Someone there?" Skinreaper whispered.
Tabitha turned around and let out a breath of relief. Nobody.

* * *

Nex yanked open the car door. He shuffled down into the passenger seat and slammed the door shut without even looking at the others. "Just fucking go!" he yelled over the same Darkthrone song playing in the car.

Throatbutcher looked in the rearview mirror. He saw Ateranimus shrugging and then stepped on the gas pedal.

The three left the red house a second time. Still without Nex's bag of amphetamine left in the studio. Which is why Nex had run back...

CHAPTER SEVEN
*B*LIP

REC 93/10/09 15:33

The studio was dimly lit with black candles. The handycam's blurry image quickly focused in on Nex tuning his guitar. His face was freshly corpsepainted. Seeing he was being filmed, he stared straight into the camera, widened his blood-shot blue eyes, bared his teeth and flipped a bird.

Skinreaper began speaking, "Hey...we've now rolled in on the fifth recording day." He filmed the song booth, which had been temporarily repaired with duct tape, and zoomed in on Throatbutcher's back. The vocalist huddled over a table, writing on a piece of paper.

He resumed his documentary narrative, "Three songs are finished and Nex is just about to lay down his evil-as-fuck guitar solo on the last one. And Throatbutcher, as you can see, is in the writing zone. Hopefully fully recovered to finish some song parts after nearly destroying half the studio...as well as my face." Skinreaper flipped the handycam around and filmed his own white-and-black painted face from above. His under lip was swollen and partly cracked. He then filmed the floor, littered with broken glass, a cracked hole in the white cement wall, broken chairs, the shattered goat skull ashtray, and finally the Marshall amp (the same one he and Tabitha had fucked on) with a guitar jammed into the grill cloth.

"Okay, I'm ready," Nex said and made the sign of the horns to the camera. He put on his headphones and shouted, "Time to raise some motherfucking hell!"

Throatbutcher shuffled past the camera and sat down by the mixer table, a spidery finger hovering over the record button.

He counted down, "Three...Two...One—"

Just as he was about to press the button a sudden bang thundered from behind as the cellar door was smashed in, knocked clean off its hinges.

Flying out of their boots, they all spun around. A giant bull moose stood on the knocked over door, furiously snorting and twitching its antlers. Lowered. Ready to attack.

"Shit!" Skinreaper gasped and staggered backwards as the brown beast, the King of the forest charged him, the hollow clattering of its hoofs against the floor resounding like sharp gunshots.

CHAPTER EIGHT

Ateranimus' gray matter stirred like whirling grain of seafloor mud. With each drop of blood drunk by the birch floor, his comatose brainstem grew stronger and stronger, jacking every neuron and synapse-thread into the wooden house.

Making it his new body. His new heart.

An old forbidden show began to perform in the theatre of his mind. Scenes wherein he lay on his mother's soft chest as her arms thrashed and slapped his smooth babyskin.

In the second act, he was crying as he listened to her comforting heartbeats as they dwindled down into infinity.

In the third and final act, the black dressed man from Ateranimus' first memory picked him up from the cooling body and held him aloft. The man's blue eyes narrowed with disgust as he stared into the infant's. Still their bond was strong. Ateranimus knew the man as his father, the same man whose teeth were bared as he put his weight on the pillow covering his mother's face.

Ateranimus roared behind the curtains of death. Fed with hatred, his heart was growing bigger. Soon, big enough to control the limbs of his new giant body. Fueled by the evil songs playing somewhere inside.

He clenched his floorboard fists, stretched his artery-fingers, and began moving forward, looking through the window which was his only eye.

Devouring everything in his way with an insatiable appetite, Ateranimus was claiming his mother's revenge. His red tinted eye locked on one building in particular...

CHAPTER NINE

Skinreaper had no chance to defend himself against the northern mastodon. The initial shock had paralyzed him, turned him into a statue of flesh. When the bull moose's gnarled antlers were close enough to gore him he came to and jumped aside—the fusty smell exuding from its fur invaded his nostrils as it brushed past him.

Throatbutcher, clutching the armrests of his swivel chair, looked like a horror version of the Munch painting "The Scream". He flew up from the seat and dodged the attacking animal by throwing himself backwards, crashing onto the 32-channel mixer. This ended in a deafening feedback as his back cranked up each channel's volume knob to max.

The infuriated bull moose rammed his antlers into the mixer table, missing Throatbutcher by inches. The horned creature easily scooped up the table with the scared shitless singer still atop of it, lifting it into the air and then dropped it just like a dipper machine dumping sand. A loud crash sounded as the piece of equipment was shattered to a pile of debris.

Throatbutcher tumbled around amid the shambles. The black eyes of the feral moose bored into him. It was now lifting its front hoofs as though trying to find a way over the rubble. And trample him to death.

In the next moment, the moose let out a bellow loud enough to be heard over the screaming feedback, as Nex drove his spiky B.C Rich guitar into the side of the animal's belly.

In one jerky move, the bull moose kneeled and pivoted around trying to bite its tormentor.

His face spattered with dark blood, Nex recoiled. The moose's teeth clacked as it snapped at Nex's nose and nearly bit it off. He winced at the sour breath that oozed from its long flabby mouth.

Suddenly, a second spatter of blood showered Nex, as a medieval flail crushed down between its antlers and smashed its eyes.

The moose dropped dead immediately and blood-soaked the fuzzy gray studio carpet. The animal didn't even make a final death-grunt.

Nex, all gored up, breathed fast. The others stood flabbergasted, with eyes like saucers.

Throatbutcher threw the weapon on the bloody carpet. Its chain rustled. He trudged over and pulled out the main plug to the PA, killing the brain-shattering feedback.

Then, a rumbling sound rose, like a rhythmic beat. Deep and ominous—as if the whole house were being lugged along the ground. Fast.

"What—the—fuck!?" Skinreaper shook his head and broke out in quick hysterical laughter. "I-I...how the hell did that fucker get in here? And what's that fucking noise?" His worried glance wandered up to the ceiling—to the creaking floorboards.

"Fuck me," screamed Nex, staring over the pile of broken equipment. "Everything... the tracks... the whole record is fucking ruined thanks to this retarded fucking moose!" His boot flew as he kicked the animal in the side.

"Shit... perhaps we can save some of it." Throatbutcher put his boot on top of the moose's antlers. He held out his balled fists and tipped his head to let his long hair flow out on his back. "Meanwhile, you can take a picture of its slayer. This could be the EP cover!"

"How do you know that you delivered the killing blow? I *stabbed* it with my guit—"

"Shit, look!" Skinreaper interrupted. His finger slowly pointed to the door-less doorway, "What the *fuck* is that?"

There, through the gap in the doorway, some fleshy membrane, marbled with blue and red veins, was spreading along the cellar interior. It was layered just like flayed skin revealing a muscular organ as it grew over the doorframe and clung to the nearby walls. Soon covering them fully like some morbid organic wallpaper.

The trio stood gawking till the strange growing film settled in and stopped expanding. They were now surrounded by the strange matter, which bristled with spidery webs of blood arteries and pumping blood vessels.

"Shit, is this some kind of biological weapon?" Skinreaper kneeled and studied the veined floor closer. "What if the world ended while we were down here?"

"I wouldn't mind," Nex circled and looked around him, "Whatever it is, I think it's fucking metal. I hate people anyway."

"Well, it ain't none of those things. Mankind has nothing to do with this," Throatbutcher said with a creepy smirk. He was staring at the ceiling, from where meaty stalactites were throbbing. "We have invoked the Dark Prince with our hymns. This is his garden. Come on, we must tell Ateranimus." He began striding toward the stairs by the broken cellar door.

Throatbutcher gasped. The steep staircase had transformed to a narrow deep red tunnel, elongated and mottled with blue cancerous patches. He ran his finger along the surface. Its texture was like the inside of a mouth. The steps were still there, but the weird membranous film had grown over them and they now jutted out like misshaped tumors. "Fascinating," he whispered and began climbing the slick bumps, ascending the blue-veined red tunnel, which seemed to have no end. Only a few crimson pinpricks could be spotted on the sides higher up.

Nex wiped gore off his face and walked to the tunnel gate. Staring up, he touched the round tunnel wall with his finger and smelled it. "Whoa, smells like raw meat…fucking awesome." He let out a crazed laugh and began climbing up, too.

Skinreaper looked at the mayhem around him. His skin began to crawl.

What the hell is happening? Did Throatbutcher lace my beer with that drug?

He rubbed his forehead and cautiously paced toward the staircase. He couldn't hear Throatbutcher and Nex's voices anymore; only that eerie rhythmic beat that seemed to sound from every nook and cranny in the house that was steadily growing into something evil.

He stared up into the abysmal tunnel and shuddered but could only see darkness. He slowly began to climb the tumorous steps, guided only by the echoes of hysteric laughter that sounded from high above.

Throatbutcher and Nex?

After some hundred steps, the steep tunnel curved sharply and Skinreaper plunged into yet another cove. He was now crawling on a plain level, and he could see the crimson light at the end. Growing bigger and bigger as he drew closer.

CHAPTER TEN

The grizzled heaven was uprising. Torrents were cast down and created a deluge of near Biblical proportions, enhanced by thunder and lightning that flashed behind the thick black smoky clouds.

But nothing would stop Ole from his life-long mission. Every atom of his body convulsed in a near orgasmic sense of righteousness. He wheeled himself faster and faster on the glistening northbound highway, defying the tempest weather, a crippled warrior. The wetness turned the asphalt into a dark mirrored strip in which he could see his own reflection; the pipe of the shotgun sticking up, the rotund outline of his face and the mighty package of his sitting body.

This powerful image fuelled him, made him strong enough to ignore the painful blisters covering his cold stiff fingers.

The past four and a half days, Ole had been weighing the pros and cons of his mission. Moral issues grinding the inside of his skull, hardly any sleep at all. And during the few hours in which he had been blessed with some, he had been plagued by the recurring nightmare: his legs shattered by the lurching black car while he was tied to a tree.

Just before the impact, he would startle awake, drenched in sweat. Fragments of sinister drunken laughter still lingered in his head. The son's of bitches escaping the grisly scene, leaving him there alone in the forest to bleed out.

A sharp splinter in the tree had been his rescue. He had used it to cut loose the tough rope, and then slithered back the several miles to Skjærfjord like a bleeding snake.

Tears now washed down his cheeks and mixed with the chilled pine-fragranced rain. After a hundred more yards of wheeling beneath the overcast sky Ole spotted the outlines of the house. It stood there, red and foreboding, deep inside the murky forest on the left side on the highway, which was now forking. He turned off from the main road and wheeled into the crude country road that would lead him to his target destination. His destiny.

The house of Hell.

Upon wheeling closer, he noticed that something was wrong with the house. Like a muscular cocoon, a film was covering the roof and half the exterior. Reddish creepers were spreading over the windows like weak bars in a mental institute.

Not ten yards from the house, he began loading his shotgun with shells from the pocket of his camouflage jacket. He did this as silently as possible, trying not to alarm the giant snorting moose standing by the porch, eating pine cones from the ground.

Come on you stupid creature, get away from the door...

The bull moose took notice of him and began scraping its hoofs in a shrub.

Ole lowered his shotgun...

Suddenly, the house's front door tore loose and flung violently into the vestibule, which obviously possessed some centrifugal force that pulled the moose, too, into its dark maw.

Ole gasped, his face twisted into fear as the wheelchair started to rattle and shake, rolling uncontrollably toward the house.

A howling, like the sound of a fierce wind, sounded from inside the house, which was changing more rapidly now. The howl drowned Ole's screams as he, along with twigs, leaves and branches snapping loose from trees, was vacuumed in through the dark gaping door-hole, one hand clutching the wheelchair and the other with a tight grip on the shotgun.

CHAPTER ELEVEN

The red tunnel was a sloping maze of twists and turns. Each crimson pinprick was a different highway leading to a different place. Distant screams and a muffled machine-like voice could be heard over the constant heart beat and howling whistle. Both noises were swaying in speed and volume, creating a nightmarish cacophony.

Throatbutcher and Nex passed one of the veined highway-tunnels, recognizing the hallway in the far end. The distance and dimness gave the optical illusion of watching the vestibule through a key-hole. They saw that a chaotic turmoil was going on in there, an electric mini-hurricane swooshing around debris.

Throatbutcher craned his neck and looked down, screaming something inaudible when a sudden headwind blew in from the hurricane-hallway. Nex, signaling that he couldn't hear a thing, motioned for him to keep climbing as the feisty gust sent small sharp twigs and leaves rasping his smeared face and blocking his sight.

They kept climbing upward, even though it was like wading through molasses, and twenty strong pulls later, as the wind finally decreased, they could escalate the final tumor-steps and climb over the slippery edge to the next level.

Nex got on his feet and looked around, wincing with pain as he removed a sprig from his ear. "Man, this is a seriously fucked up garden..."

"Yes, isn't it," Throatbutcher snickered. "You expected pink roses?"

The crimson hall they were standing in had walls of throbbing muscular tissue that were held in place with sinewy threads. Embedded in them, were three arched, six-foot tall entrances covered by the same gelatinous and veined membrane as in the cellar.

"Come on!" Throatbutcher said and punched through the membrane door closest to him. He stepped into it, and the moment he entered he let out a raspy wheeze, "He's awake!"

"What!?" Nex called and frowned as he hurried after. His pulse racing with anticipation as he first glimpsed Throatbutcher's back behind the membrane door. He appeared to be kneeling on the floor. *Why?*

Nex took one more step, nearly shitting himself as he saw *what* it was Throatbutcher was kneeling before.

"Holy fuck!" Nex yelled, his brain about to pop.

For there, in the same room they had conducted the ritual earlier, Ateranimus' corpse was sliced to hundreds of strings running from the bed and up to the ceiling where they connected with his flat face, scraped high up there like a disc of melted flesh.

Overall, the unholy creation looked like a cross between a marionette doll and pinkish bubblegum stuck between the sole of your shoe and the curb. Thready. And as the visual shock settled, the olfactory aftershock flew through the air like a putrid jet plane.

"Fuck!" Nex gagged, his hand covering his nose, "that's...that's *him*?"

Laughing madly, Throatbutcher turned and grinned at Nex who stood a bit behind him, "In the flesh! He's talking to me, I can hear him so loud and clear... like crystal!"

Completely stunned, Nex's wide eyes took in the ceiling. Especially the area around Ateranimus' distorted pancake-face, where a black fungus was spreading rapidly over the complex artery threadwork which was expanding and shrinking. Beating strongly as the veins fed the thirsty wood with blood.

"Okay...?" Swallowing, Nex spoke slowly in a monotonous tone, "what's he saying...?"

"Shhhh..." Throatbutcher put a finger over his crusted black lipstick and closed his eyes. "Friends are not what they seem."

Suddenly, Nex startled as a faint demonic breath seemed to whisper his name through the walls of muscled flesh...

CHAPTER TWELVE

The late October afternoon was being whipped by an extreme overcast. Tabitha was just passing the green road sign saying *Bjørkefjord 10* when her car engine suddenly decided to die on her.

"You gotta be kidding me..." Groaning, she slammed her hands against the steering wheel in frustration, "fucking *fuck*!"

She pulled over to the side of the wet road just in time before the car jerked to a halt with a mechanical death rattle.

"Oh, this is just perfect. Fucking piece of *shit!*" She let her head fall back on the seat and yanked out the keys from the ignition. The pentagram keychain jangled.

She stared out through the rainy windshield, weighing her options. Slim pickings.

Further ahead she could spot the Texaco where she had tanked up just before the band meeting nearly a week ago. The one with the creepy clerk. Unfortunately, it seemed to be closed. The red-white star was dead.

"Great..."

It wasn't like she could walk the remaining distance to the house. Not with her high-heels and especially not in the heavy downpour. Hitch-hiking was out of the question. Hard when there are no cars out on the road.

On a great day, maybe one or two vehicles drove the desolate Skjærfjord-Bjørkefjord route. The twin towns were like Siamese twins. People found excuses not to come by. And even if a car did pass, chances were non-existent they would pick up a twenty-something-girl with black hair reaching to her hips dressed in slutty black clothes cluttered with patches of pentagrams and inverted crosses.

No. She would just have to suck it up and walk the distance.

She was snatching her cell from the dashboard when three hard knocks suddenly rapped the car window. Jumping in her seat, she dropped the phone and saw the rain blurred face of a man looking in on her from the outside.

Jeez! Scared the shit outta me...

Another knock came, lighter this time.

"Must be my lucky day," Tabitha muttered while rolling down the window. The forty-something, kind-faced man had bushy blonde hair sticking out from under his red trucker-cap. The cap bore a print of two hands making the thumbs-up sign and a white text reading: I'm "*that*" guy!

Sure are, sucker...

"Car problem?" the man asked in a sprightly tone with a toothy grin. Raindrops were dripping from his pointy nose down to his dry lips where he caught them with his tongue.

"Um, yes. Looks that way," Tabitha offered him a sheepish grin.

The man let out a hearty chuckle. He pointed with both his hands at his cap and raised his light brows, making big eyes, as if he had just told a joke and was awaiting his audience to get it.

"Eh, what?" Tabitha replied with a confused frown. Irritation was climbing inside her.

"I'm *that* guy!" He laughed out and clapped his hands. "Don't you see? I'm that guy, who will help you with a ride into town. That is if you don't mind a little smell. I've filled her up with a load of freshly caught salmon. Norway's best!" He pointed at his box-car parked not far behind.

He's just a harmless fisherman. Not likely he'll rape or murder me...

"Well, sure. Thanks." Tabitha shot him a tight smile and gathered her stuff.

"No problem. Always happy to help a *damsel in distress*." He winked and jogged back to his fish-truck.

Tabitha got out of her car and jogged toward his truck, her small purse over her head trying to avoid the ice cold skyfall that was soaking her. As she climbed in, her daring outfit clung to her body like a second skin.

As she sat down in the passenger seat of the fish-truck, her ears were invaded by Bjørn Eidsvåg's pastoral voice blaring from the car radio, apparently tuned in on some Christian music channel. And *that guy* wasn't lying, the fish stench was overpowering and almost made her gag.

Tabitha took a deep breath and silently wished she could magically turn off her ears and nose.

The trucker grinned at her and offered his big hand, "Kåre's the name."

Tabitha looked at his hand sprinkled with fish-scales and reluctantly shook it. She caught him stealing a dirty glance at her deep décolletage—her nipples were poking out of her wet black top like two golf pegs. She crossed her arms and stared straight ahead.

Kåre cleared his throat and revved the fish-truck which rolled onward at a leisurely speed; slowly chewing up the ten mile strip of glassy asphalt.

CHAPTER THIRTEEN

Skinreaper had crept toward the crimson light and was now standing in a small remote corner of what used to be their kitchen. Now, it was a dismal chamber wherein every straight angle had been twisted into soft and bulbous tumors. The palpitating room was draining his sense of balance, the same way a house of mirrors would.

The only source of light, and overall normalcy in the narrow room, came from a single window to the left. Even that had changed and was now tinted red by some slithering creepers growing over the glass from the outside. Like gnarled blood-stained bars in a surreal prison.

He staggered toward it and peered out, "No..." he gasped.

The house was moving. Pulled forward by those scarlet creepers, each one branching off into thin fingers with small mouths where nails should've been, consuming everything in their way. As if the house had become some kind of animated organic machine, a huge mutated vessel of wood and muscle...

What made the bad situation even worse, was that the wood-muscle vessel was moving toward Bjørkefjord. Like a fucked-up version of Titanic, in which the house was playing the infamous ocean liner, and the town, taking on the demanding role of the iceberg. He knew how that shit ended.

Vaguely through the bars, he could also see the townspeople gathered in front of the house horizon like an army of ants, armed with rifles, sledge hammers and even some burning torches. On the far edge of the little village stood the white church steeple jutting up, like a mother swan watching over its cygnets.

Shit, looks like the Skjærfjorders won't give up without a good fight.

His brain worked on the double to come up with an escape plan. He looked around in search for a weapon. He needed guns or a fucking bazooka but could only find mundane kitchen stuff: cutlery, glassware, plates, and the coffee machine that was melting into the wall but was rejected by the picky flesh. He stared dejectedly up at the ceiling. He knew that Ateranimus room was on the other side. He could even pick up Throatbutcher and Nex's faint muffled voices up there.

How the hell am I supposed to get through? Fuck!

The constant grinding of the house advancing added to the panic building up inside.

"Hey! Can you hear me?" Skinreaper yelled at the ceiling. "We must get out of here! The house is...fuck it, they can't hear me..."

He spotted a big knife sitting in the soft wall. He pulled it out and wiped off the gore on his Venom t-shirt and hauled his ass up on the kitchen counter. At this height he could reach the slick ceiling.

Here we go...

Skinreaper began stabbing the ceiling with the knife. Jets of blood squirted down on him with each incision and a deep tormenting wail sounded from somewhere. It made his neck hair stand on its ends. Wiping off the constant leaking of blood that showered his face, he focused on cutting loose some threads of sinew as well as a good sized gash in the meat.

Retching from the iron tasting blood he accidentally swallowed, he keeled over to throw up but managed to focus on his breathing and held it in.

The sinew threads were tough, like cutting trough thick leather. But persistence and years of drumming was steadily getting him there. Within a minute, a big wedge of meat hung loose. Big enough to get his hands into the cleft and rip open a wide passageway. He dropped the knife, grabbed hold of a hanging sinew thread and began climbing it like a rope.

Skinreaper pushed his head through the cut-up slit in the ceiling. He felt a surge of hope when spotting the backs of his band members. He heaved his whole body through the tear, pushed his weight over the edge and plopped onto his back on the slippery floor.

"We must get the hell outta here, the house is, is... it'll collide with the town!" Skinreaper's words came out strained. He rolled over on his side and wiped off a strand of bile drooling from his parched lips.

"Yes. We know. Ateranimus had some unfinished business to take care of..." It was Nex who dropped the strange remark.

"What?" Skinreaper said and turned while getting up on his feet.

That's when he saw the morbid marionette—Ateranimus post-mortem—consisting now of billowing veins sprouting from the bed and feeding blood to a giant throbbing tumor growing from the ceiling. Molded into the shape of Ateranimus' head, its breathing was like white noise.

Skinreaper shot backwards, "What the hell is *that*?"

"You remember Ateranimus? His appearance has changed a bit since you last saw him. But I assure you, he's still the same sweet guy as before. So, no need to leave so soon." Throatbutcher sneered. He was standing by the bed, gripping a long black leather whip in his hands.

Nex stood beside him with a coy smirk on his face.

A giant pentagram was cut into the flesh-floor in front of them, separating them from Skinreaper. Dark blood was seeping out from the crude carvings.

"What's going on guys?" Skinreaper said and frowned, an awkward vibe creeping over him like a cold shadow. "Have I missed something?"

Throatbutcher lowered his head, his dark eyes still locked on Skinreaper. He began to circle the whip over the floor, like a coiling snake.

Nex let out a quiet laughter and slowly approached Skinreaper with his fists balled.

Skinreaper backed off but was quickly cornered. He leaned back a little, shaking his head. "What are you doing?" His eyes felt hot from the threat.

Nex didn't reply but kept advancing, his face now only an inch away from Skinreaper's.

"Hey, lay off," Skinreaper snapped and raised his hands to chin level.

Nex shot a dirty look at him and started sniffing. "Is that fear I smell?" He crinkled his nose and discharged a gob of spittle landing on top of Skinreaper's boot. "You afraid of me?"

"Dude, this is ridiculous, what's your fucking prob—"

"You afraid to die?" Nex cut him off with a lopsided smile, "I always knew you were a fucking poser..."

Before Skinreaper could reply, a bouquet of white fractal flowers suddenly exploded inside his skull and drained his field of vision. He could hear Throatbutcher's vile laughter echoing and he realized that Nex had clocked him with a headbutt.

He tasted blood in his mouth as he began crawling up on his feet. His nose felt like numb pounding potato. In the corner of his eye he saw Nex approach him once more, this time loading up to kick him in the face.

"This one's for fucking Tab..."

Skinreaper winced in advance; holding his hands up to shield his face.

"Don't!" Throatbutcher ordered and held his whip-hand up like a mighty emperor. "Leave the impostor to his own fate. We have more important things to tend too. We have to focus, it's very close now."

Nex aborted his kick and took a step back, cracking his fingers. His breathing was steamed up.

Throatbutcher proceeded, "We must make sure Ateranimus' revenge is carried out against his father. No room for fuckups."

A static jagged laughter sounded from Ateranimus enormous tumor-face. It began to throb faster, appearing to almost burst with stirred excitement. Its black tongue writhing in and out of its cancer mouth, licking its tarry lips.

"You're fucking crazy!" Skinreaper rubbed blood off his face and staggered toward the cut-up slit in the floor. "Do what the hell you want—I'm leaving!" he yelled while climbed back through it and slid down the sinew liana.

Back in the kitchen, he could hear Throatbutcher scream, "In the name of all the Lords of the Abyss, I call out to the Powers of Darkness!"

A fit of cold sweat broke out on Skinreaper's slimy face as he stared through the barred red window once more. The cataclysmic collision was very close now, a minute or two if he were lucky.

Suddenly, the glass window shattered in a thousand pieces accompanied with rapid staccato gunfire.

"Shit shit shit!" Skinreaper screamed as he ducked and jogged toward the mouth of the tunnel. "Please let there be a way out..."

From the upstairs he could hear Ateranimus' uncanny phantom voice, calling out an invocation together with Throatbutcher, "Hear me Lord Satan! I am persecuted on all sides. My enemies hem me in and would set out to cut me off. They would deny me goods and services because I serve thee, O Dark Prince!"

Skinreaper escaped through the tunnel. His brain was desperately trying to save him from going batshit. But logic was lost. The surreal truth was slowly cracking him, one flake of sanity at a time.

So I've seen Ateranimus giant rotten head growing out from the fucking ceiling. Even saw his brain wired to the house like junk inside the chassis of a car. But what *is the motor making the house move?*

Warm blood from his nose was stinging his cracked lips and the blue artery webs inside the red tunnel flashed by his flickering eyes, when the answer dawned on him.

Oh, my god, it's a heart...and I'm crawling in it!

CHAPTER FOURTEEN

Ole shook awake to the sounds of muffled chanting, hysterical laughter and strange bassy heartbeats.

"Holy mother of God..." Ole's eyes slowly adjusted to the dim light of the red pulsating room. It was soft-cornered, with blue-veined walls. It smelled like funky meat. He steeled himself to keep his stomach contents down.

The moose. The front door being sucked into the house. The accidental shot that went off and hit the moose in its belly, and the strange electric hurricane swooping him up, tossing him like a glove through a dark tunnel. Then....nothing.

The room itself was almost empty save for some black plastic bags sitting in a corner. Dust-caked stereo equipment and broken speakers were stacked in another. Lying on his stomach, Ole spotted the shotgun next to his wheelchair, which had tipped over on one of its wheels.

He began hauling his limp body toward his handicap vehicle, when he suddenly heard running footsteps drawing closer. He faced the sound. It came from behind a strange looking passageway covered with a membranous see-through film that was dangling in scraps as if burst. Probably from him flying through it.

Ole picked up speed and grabbed hold of the shotgun in the next pull. He rolled over on his back and fished out shells from his jacket's breast pocket, pushing them into the loading flap with his thumb.

Squinting, he held his breath and pointed the loaded gun in the direction of the opening. His heart was beating fast, in sync with the heartbeat of the house. There was a sudden darkening of the eerie reddish light just before the running stranger entered the room.

"Stop right there asshole!" Ole yelled. He tried to sound mean but his awkward position on the floor only made him sound weak. "Hands against the wall. Now!"

Ole recognized the man as the band's drummer, Skinpeeper or Skinleaper: a short muscular guy with a pointed face, bleeding piggy nose and long thick black hair in a big mess.

"Shit! Don't shoot!" Skinreaper raised his hands. The legless, beady-eyed psycho sprawled on the floor, aiming the big shotgun at his face. "Who the hell are you!?"

"Hands, wall, now!"

Skinreaper turned and placed his hands on the flesh-wall, panic rushing inside him like a derailing locomotive. "Listen! This house will crash into the town any second now and I'm not planning on being in it when it does. So, please, whoever you are and whatever your problem is, just let me get the fuck outta here. Okay!?"

The crippled gunman squinted, "My name is not important. I'm here to collect a debt from your little black metal buddies. A debt that is way overdue." Ole used one hand to back up against the tipped-over wheelchair, knocked it back up and hauled himself into the seat.

Skinreaper squirmed in his boots. His face glowed red with frustration. "Look! I know nothing about any debt, or what the hell you're talking about, so I'm gonna go now. Shoot me if you want," he began pacing out of the room with his hands clasped behind his neck, "I'd prefer getting my head blown to pieces to being inside when this fucking heart ruptures."

Ole gritted his teeth. He had not expected this reaction. But he couldn't pull the trigger against an innocent man. And now his hostage, his only ticket to finding the true enemies, was escaping out the hallway tunnel.

"Wait!" Ole screamed after him trying to wheel himself forward. "Just tell me where they are!" The dull flesh-floor made it impossible to roll forward even an inch. "Piece of shit wheelchair!" He slung the shotgun over his back, hauled himself over the seat and plopped down onto the meaty surface.

He moved like a worm over the slippery floor. He was determined they wouldn't get away with their heinous deed. It didn't matter if he died from the coming impact. As long as he didn't die before snuffing out the assholes responsible for his misery.

I will find you, and when I do, I'll shoot your fucking legs off...

Just as he passed the membrane passageway and slithered out into the hallway, the voice of the previous hostage shouted from somewhere not far, "Take the tunnel upstairs!"

Ole saw what must be the tunnel referred to. Like a viper on fire, he writhed toward the end of the hallway. The closer he got, the more distinct the chanting voices upstairs became. One of them, the laughing idiot, was a dead giveaway. It was the same maniacal guffaw he had heard the evening of the 'accident'. There was also a third voice, deep and ominous, that he didn't recognize.

Don't worry, I never forget a face.

Ole looked up at the dark and steep tunnel. The steps looked like inflamed lesions covered with flecks of blood. He drew a sheath knife from his belt and stabbed it hard into the tissue. A puddle of viscous black fluid bubbled up around the blade.

Groaning from the exertion, Ole dragged his body up and steadily began climbing his morbid Mount Everest, at which top he would finally seal his destiny and receive eternal serenity...

CHAPTER FIFTEEN

"There! She's one of Satan's minions! Get her!" The outcry came from the crowd of townspeople, waving and pointing their fingers at Tabitha who was climbing out of the fish-truck that had parked by the blue REMA 1000 grocery store in the center of town.

Seconds earlier, she had heard several gunshots and now a big lynch mob, armed with sledge hammers and torches flickering in the rainy gray dusk, came swarming in from around the corner, moving directly toward the truck.

As she threw her high heels and looked back at the angry flock approaching her, she glimpsed the gargantuan black meat-monster, pumping and growing as it sucked in houses into a giant purplish artery, as if they were little Monopoly properties.

Tabitha lost her grip on reality. Everything felt like a slow wave, her ears started ringing and her mouth tasted electric cotton.

This is not real. I'm having a nervous breakdown...

She ran faster but the ground around her seemed to wither before her bare feet. Her tunnel vision registered the white brick church not far ahead, sheltered by a row of pastel colored houses. She staggered toward the soup of gaudy squares, strangely thinking her own bed was in one of them.

The sounds of the mob were drawing closer. The raw October wind carried yells and terrified screams, gunshots and barking dogs.

Then Tabitha felt her legs turn to jelly and she collapsed on an unkempt lawn. The moment before she passed out, she saw a shadow looming over her. As her eyes rolled in their sockets, she saw that the shadow belonged to a strong-jawed man, balding with gray tufts of hair.

She recognized him. But from where? Then she knew.

Ateranimus' father...

* * *

When Tabitha awoke she couldn't move. Her neck felt sore and her mouth was dry. Ropes held her in place, cutting into her wrists and ankles. She craned her neck and found that she was tied to a red velvet clad altar in front of a six-foot tall wooden cross with Jesus nailed to it. Stifling heat came from hundreds of lit white candles surrounding her. Cherubim coated in gold leered at her from the ceiling, innocently plucking their miniature lyres.

Even though it was quiet inside the church, she picked up the mayhem going on outside. Muffled screams and car alarms bleeping. Like an urban war fought on low volume.

Shit, was that monster for real?

She quickly began working the ropes by moving her arms and legs back and forth. Her captor had done a shitty job tying her up. She flinched as she heard a sudden man's voice behind her—

"You knew Henriette was a whore the first time you looked into her eyes." The speaker was clearly talking to himself since Tabitha had no fucking idea who this Henriette was.

He began to sob, "A sinner...Why did you let her drag you down to her carnal pit of sin? Oh, why?"

Oh, yeah—Ateranimus' father, the priest.

She decided to keep silent and play it smart. Play dead.

"But I purged my sin! Hear me, God! I purged my sin when I killed the whore!" His voice dwindled down to a near guttural tone. "...I should have killed the spawn of her womb too. But because of my weakness, that seed of Satan...my evil boy...has now returned in his true shape to bring forth death upon us all..."

Just as Tabitha had freed her left hand she heard a sharp metallic ring, like the blade of a knife against a rough surface. Then she saw the shadow of the black dressed priest in the corner of her eye.

"God! I beg you to forgive my mistake! Accept this sacrifice! Reward me for cutting off Satan's hellish limbs!"

Cold sweat exploded in Tabitha's face as she fumbled to loosen the rope on her right hand. The priest was now right by her side. His eyes closed and his breath became more and more excited. He slowly raised a glinting silver dagger into the air. The flickering flames of the candles reflected in the blade like little white nails.

Just as the priest was about to thrust the holy knife into her chest, something interrupted his sacrifice. Sadly, it wasn't angels that had come to her rescue.

The monster's here...

An earthquake-like tremor shook the ground, shattering every glass window inside the church. The low war sounds were rapidly escalating into a concentrated mass of screams.

"Judgment Day..." the priest whispered and quickly raised the dagger again. His eyes were wide and his mouth half open as though both fascinated and repulsed by his coming move.

A deafening squeal suddenly filled the high dome. The priest dropped the knife on the stone floor where it landed with a sharp clang. His face contorted with pain as he staggered backwards cupping his crotch.

"I think my nails got stuck in your dress, bitch!" Tabitha grinned as she began to untie the rope around her feet.

"You whore of Satan!" the priest wheezed out. He grabbed an iron candelabrum next to him and began wielding it like a sword while shuffling towards Tabitha.

Free at last, Tabitha knocked over some candles as she jumped over to the left side of the altar, using it to separate herself from the priest. She misjudged the size of the candelabra that came swinging at her in a wide arc and hit her over the cheek with a loud crack. She hit the floor and landed badly on her arm, yelping as spears of white fire shot through it. Spitting out blood and a handful of teeth, she rose back up on her feet and started running toward the church doors.

The priest had now rallied himself into a psychotic state of mind, "God, please don't punish me," he wailed as he set after her.

The church floor had started to crack up, rupturing under the violent trembling that intensified with each second. Tabitha held her breath, expecting the whole building to collapse at any moment. The farthest pews, the altar, and even the huge crucifix were now torn from the floor, flying out through the arched openings of the broken windows.

Only two more steps, please, please let me make it!

Just as Tabitha rammed her side into the sturdy double door, she felt the priest's strong arm. A chokehold.

"Got you!"

Her hands flew up, gripping the arm around her neck, trying to break free. But he was too strong. With every passing second she could feel her lungs shrink. Gasping for air, she managed to tilt her head back just as the whole wall of the church disappeared, each white brick whirling into the artery tube of the black heart.

Tabitha's face was now the tone of a pale plum, her teary eyes bulging, when she saw a dozen of scarlet tendrils, each the size of a manila rope, suddenly shoot out from the giant heart and wind around the priest's throat.

Screaming, he released his chokehold on Tabitha and desperately tried to pull them off. But the tendrils kept coiling and twisting around each other, till they were covering his whole face. A sickening crunching was heard as the capillary threads crushed his skull, then, just as quickly as they had darted in, retracted back with one fierce pull, yanking the priest with them.

With one hand on the door handle and another holding her burning throat, Tabitha keeled over.

Then the whole church floor collapsed, presenting a vast black smoking chasm underneath. The marble floor bricks tumbled down. A seismic roar came from the black heart monster as it shambled over the ruined church and bored itself down into the vast burrow.

CHAPTER SIXTEEN

Panting, Ole came crawling into the crimson cave hallway just as the tunnel behind clogged up with fat sickly yellow pus. The heart, as his hostage had called it, had clearly entered the state of rupture. Downstairs, he heard loud crashes, as if somebody was going berserk and tossing large pieces of furniture around. The whole house was careening, shaking and gliding.

Ole ignored it. His focus was directed on the ripped membrane door from where the voices came. He had thought he would fear the Grand Finalé. But he did not. His hands were steady.

Shotgun first, he slithered toward the opening like an FSK soldier. He lowered his head, heart pounding with excitement, as he reached the soft threshold and peered into the dark room. He wasn't prepared for what lay inside...

"Holy fucking mother of God," he whispered.

Rope thick blood veins hanging from the ceiling were wrapped around a big ash-colored tumor that rotated like a hundred-kilo pig on an electric spit. The tumor was sculptured like a face, with a pointed nose and a set of deep hollow eye-sockets. A thick black sausage tongue lolled out from its livery lips, now and then wetting them with viscous purple spittle. Sudden bursts of jagged static grunts came from it.

Swallowing, Ole let his narrow eyes wander to a tiny window by which the duo of corpsepainted culprits from the past stood looking out.

Seeing their black shocks of hair sharing the space of the window, Ole thought of two guys watching the Winter Olympics, gesturing wildly, hooting and howling over whatever it was they saw on the outside.

Ole's flustered face melted into a sinister grin. His gaze darkened and locked on them as if they were two rare black bears and he a big game hunter.

If I survive the rupture, I'll nail your heads onto plaques and hang them on my wall like trophies...

Ole salivated. He gently squeezed the cold metal of the trigger...

* * *

"Fucking hell! This is awesome!" Nex yelled, watching through the window as the giant purple artery sucked everything in its way: disintegrating the bricks of houses, crumbling the streets like cookies. He let out a war whoop for each and every Christian flung into the tube like tiny ants being snorted by an ant-eater.

Throatbutcher was a little bit more composed. Heightened. He felt like an emperor of death staring out at the mayhem created before them, accomplished for succeeding with the invocation that had empowered Ateranimus' phantom being: the black heart. Ateranimus' mind was linked to his own, a means of communication between the two as they navigated toward the final target. The church.

So close now...if only I had brought a spoon of that drug to enhance this!

Throatbutcher raised his arms and bowed his head, letting his dark hair fall over his face like black velvet curtains as he said, "The damaged peace nurtures the jelly..."

BANG!

Throatbutcher's skull and brain splash-painted the window and part of the wall a deeper shade of crimson.

A rumbling, ululating roar sounded from the rotating tumor head which began to convulse in violent spasms. The house's heartbeats began to race like the clattering hoofs of a runaway horse.

The final rupture...

Coated with gore and pieces of Throatbutcher, Nex spun around, when he saw the crippled sniper aiming at him...

CHAPTER SEVENTEEN

Skinreaper had to creep along the wall not to be picked up by the electric hurricane in the hallway, emanating from a huge black hole in the floor. On tenterhooks, he crossed the thin ledge of floor still left, whirling leaves and pine cones brushing his face as he lurched into the vestibule.

The front door was gone but still impassable. The red creepers growing over the windows covered the doorway too.

"Shit!"

Skinreaper grabbed a shoehorn still hanging on a coat rack in a desperate attempt to try severing the mucous cords. He felt a twang of hope as they slowly but steadily split up one by one, oozing out rank coppery blood that danced around on the pumping meat.

FTHOMP... FTHOMP... FTHOMP... FTHOMP... FTHOMP... FTHOMP...

The thumping came in rapid succession, each catch accompanied by a choir of tormented wails. Then the heart began convulsing and chugging. Skinreaper was knocked off his feet and landed head first in the pool of dancing blood.

His nails dug into the meat wall as he tried to get up, spitting out the evil-tasting fluid. Slipping and sliding in the goo, trying to find his balance, he heard the unexpected sound of churning waves drawing close.

Drunkenly, he turned his head and saw a tsunami rolling toward him. The mighty waves grew from a slushy sea of blood, a high deep-red crest sprinkled with broken bones and foaming with body fluids and teeth. Lapping in slow motion.

As the first drop tickled his nose, Skinreaper grabbed hold of a gashed artery-creeper. His eyes bugged and his cheeks ballooned as he took a big gulp of air, preparing for the gory deluge.

Then he bathed...

* * *

Skinreaper swung and swayed, pretending he was algae and flowers clinging to a reef. It was almost beautiful. Swirly crimson currents and pink crystal bubbles. White bricks, water pipes, shingles, and furniture gently bumped into him. Now and then, severed heads with faces twisted in gruesome expressions came floating by as if to greet him, hair flowing like jellyfish. An eyeball with the nerve tail still attached to it swam around like some exotic shrimp.

Suddenly, the creeper he was holding onto snapped loose, and in one immense rush he shot out of the heart and tumbled onto the ground. Rejected, like the fourth metal in an alloy.

* * *

It was cold and dark outside. Fetal positioned, Skinreaper lay in a shallow puddle of gore. Far ahead, the black heart was boring itself into the ground, flinging dollops of mud as it went deeper and deeper, bawling like a demonic infant calling for its succubus mother.

The last thing to sink down into the abysmal hollow was a six-foot tall crucifix on which Jesus Christ stared up toward the black heaven, as if imploring his old man to save him.

Next moment, he was swallowed by the Earth.

Skinreaper laughed at the irony and slowly rose to his feet. Enveloped by a strange silence, he looked around and noticed the whole town was gone. As if it had never been there.

Like the last man on Earth, he began pacing forward in no particular direction. After three steps his strength ran out and he collapsed in a pile of crumbled bricks. His tired eye noticed an alpine-white mouse nibbling on a finger that it held within its tiny hands. Noticing it was being watched, the mouse stared back with its red eyes and scurried away with the finger.

Skinreaper was just about to fall into a hundred hour sleep when he saw the shape of a woman emerging from the dusty darkness, wisps of black hair dancing in the wind.

He mustered a weary smile and she offered the same.

Skinreaper giggled.

The woman's mouth was a mess, several of her teeth were missing...

Michael Faun is a writer of weird fiction. Beside his latest short fiction collection "Six Pack o' Strange Tales" from Sigil Press, he has stories published in anthologies such as "Witches!" from Dynatox Ministries, "Ugly Babies" and "Indiana Horror Review 2013", both from James Ward Kirk Publishing. He lives with his wife and daughter in a decrepit Swedish coastal town where he enjoys everything trash culture: books, comics and movies. He also dabbles in spicy vodouesque cooking and rumor has it, he was once nearly blinded by ghost pepper chili. To find out more about him and read free stuff go to: **http://michaelfaun.wordpress.com**

Printed in Great Britain
by Amazon